A Mystery In White

The Lakeside Cozy Cat Mystery Series
Book 2

D1715903

JANET EVANS

FREE!

Grab One Hour Free Of An Exciting Audiobook Now!

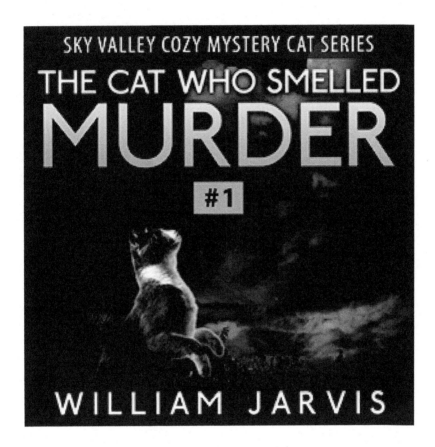

VISIT THE LINK BELOW NOW:
http://clika.pe/l/10263/27051/

Janet Evans

Yap Kee Chong

8345 NW 66 ST #B7885

Miami, FL 33166

Paperback Edition

Copyright 2016

CHAPTER 1

Susan Becker slipped into her gently worn terry cloth robe after stepping out of the shower. Though the cold tile of her master bathroom floor always sent a shiver through her, she rarely remembered to take the preventative step of bringing her slippers into the bathroom for her morning showers. She treated her icy feet to the welcoming warmth of her plush and fuzzy red bath mat. It was the bit of whimsy that had somehow found its way into Susan's heart to disrupt the black and white world that had been her bathroom. After this addition a year ago, various splashes of red had gradually invaded the space from red towels to a bright red toothbrush holder. Susan considered her morning ablutions to be more ritual than obligation, so she never rushed through them even though it meant waking at a painfully early hour to start her baking by 3:30 am. As soon as she felt finally prepared to face the day, Susan ventured out of her master bathroom toward the closet that lay across an ocean of gray colored carpet. At least once a week, she promised herself she would take this horrid carpet up because it was almost the exact same color as her feline companion's fur, therefore making him almost completely camouflaged. No sooner had she made this promise again when she stumbled over his soft and furry body directly impeding his course. Mr. Giles' drowsy green eyes looked up at her accusingly, as if to say, "Why are you kicking me? Don't you see I'm trying to sleep?"

Susan kept an eye warily upon him as she continued making her way to the cramped closet near her 4-poster bed. On the other hand, Mr. Giles had lost interest in his human roommate, instead he had immediately settled back into a peaceful slumber. She donned a pair of jeans and a T-shirt that was more uniform than outfit, then started for the bedroom door. Before she turned off the light and left the room, Susan paused as she stole one last glance at Mr. Giles. She felt a twinge of envy as she left him slumbering while she was off to prepare for the 7a.m. opening of her bakery. With a sigh, she slipped on her house shoes and flicked the switch.

Susan had found that every non-carpeted surface felt frigid at this hour of the day, no matter the season. So she was grateful for the protection her house slippers provided on the hardwood floors while she made her way down the narrow hallway to the kitchen. It was difficult for her to focus on baking for her patrons before she had eaten anything herself, so breakfast was a high priority. Susan was soon immersed in the calm blues and greens of her kitchen décor. She rummaged around in her refrigerator until she had two eggs and a bag of extra sharp cheddar cheese in hand. While she was scrambling the eggs, she pulled some salsa and tortillas out of the fridge. Barely ten minutes had gone by before she had put two piping hot breakfast burritos in a small plastic dish, snapped the lid shut, and headed out the door.

While munching on her burritos, she meandered down the creaky wooden steps which led from her front door directly into her small bakery. The ovens warmed up in her commercial kitchen and Susan pulled some overnight batters out of the refrigerator. Doughnuts, muffins, and cinnamon rolls were always an expectation for the breakfast crowd. By 6:30a.m, she had all of these best sellers waiting in their trays. Susan left them covered and on top of the stove for a few more minutes. It was a trick she had learned to keep the treats warm while they were waiting for the shop to open. Skimping on details like that could jeopardize her reputation for having the best baked goods in town.

After sliding a few more tasty selections into the oven to bake, she exited the swinging doors from the kitchen to the shop. On the back counter sat three large pots of coffee, two with brown tops and one with an orange top. From the cabinet below, she removed the packages of regular and decaf coffee, and then set all of the pots to brew. Absentmindedly, she had grabbed a rag and started to wipe down her counters and display cases, though they were already clean from the day before. This was the part of the morning routine that Susan found most tedious. While she busied herself turning on all the lights and filling up the cash register, Mr. Giles strolled into the room to join her. They made the rest of the rounds together until 6:59 arrived. Susan flipped her sign from closed to open then went back behind the counter to help herself to a cup of coffee before any customers arrived. In her opinion coffee was best when it was chock full of cream and sugar to mask its bitter flavor. On this occasion she made liberal use of a delicious Butter Pecan flavored creamer so she could have a full dose of caffeine without any unpleasant coffee taste.

It was 7:12 and no one had come in yet. It wasn't that surprising to have a slow day in early August, the summer tourist season in Lakeside, MO was winding down. But there were still things going on around town this week and most kids weren't back to school yet, so she thought she might get some local travelers in today. The thing with travelers from nearby towns is that they usually don't come in the shop first thing in the morning. After all, they were on vacation, why should they get up at dawn? Her mind drifted from the vacation plans of her customers to wistful thoughts of her own vacation plans. She imagined herself lazily sleeping in before venturing out to explore some new and exciting place. It had been awhile since she had been on vacation and the places that she hoped to visit continued to accrue with the passage of time. Just as she was envisioning herself at the Louvre, her daydream was interrupted by the jingling of the bell on her door signaling the arrival of her first customer of the day.

It was Kip Fletcher, Lakeside's finest police detective, at least in Susan's humble opinion. The fact that he was easy on the eyes didn't hurt either. Though not your classic tall and chiseled type that many women found attractive, Kip's features had a boyish quality that melted her heart. He sauntered over to the bar stool nearest to the rectangular glass display cases which made up half of the front counter space. "Good morning, Suzie. What smells so good?"

"Everything's good here, you know that. "

"Well I've got my eye on those blueberry muffins," he pointed to them in the case next to him. "Tell me something. Are they half as sweet as the woman who made them?"

"Well, they're at least half, "she answered with a wink.

He smiled broadly in response, then leaned across the counter and looked into her eyes. "Well, I can't pass up anything that sweet. So I'll take two."

Susan turned her attention quickly to the display case, so Kip wouldn't notice that she was blushing. She slid two blueberry muffins off of aluminum tray in the display case. The plates were in the cabinet behind her, she was relieved for yet another reason to avoid eye contact. She placed the muffins on an ivory collared plastic plate, then slid them across the counter to the detective. "Would you like a cup of coffee with that?"

"Sure," he agreed amicably. "You know how I like it."

She did indeed. She'd shared enough meals with Kip to know exactly how he liked his coffee. She poured him a cup in a porcelain mug and since he was the only customer there so far, she fixed it up just as he would like before setting it next to his plate.

After taking his first few bites and murmuring his satisfaction, he began sipping his coffee contemplatively. His attention was obviously elsewhere as his facial expression had become quite perplexed. Kip's job was to investigate homicides and missing persons. Susan figured he must have a new case.

"I have to tell you, Sue, this latest case is really a strange one."

"Do you want to talk about it?"

"You know the circus is in town, right? Well, it seems that someone broke in early this morning to steal their white Bengal tiger. During the commission of this crime, one of their security guards was murdered. He had a mark on his neck, which the medical examiner says looks like an injection mark. We don't know yet if killing the guard was part of the plan or if things just went sideways."

"A missing tiger?! Who would steal a tiger?"

"No clue." Kip returned his attention to his muffins. "Right now, I don't know why anybody would want to steal a tiger. And, honestly, I don't know who could steal a tiger, even if they did want to."

"That is a valid point," Susan conceded. "So you don't have a motive?"

"Well, I wouldn't say that exactly. Until I find out differently, I'm assuming money is the motive. I don't really know how much a white Bengal tiger might fetch on the black market. But I'm willing to guess that it's a pretty penny."

"I would agree with that assessment." ~~To Susan this seemed to be neither.~~

"The mayor is very upset over this thing. You know how he feels about anything that affects tourism or revenue. And since we have closed every case that we've opened this year, he called me personally about this case."

Susan couldn't help but wonder who Kip was including in the "we" who solved every case this year. Certainly she and Mr. Giles had been just as instrumental to solving the cases as Detectives Kip Fletcher and Frank Matthews had been. But she didn't investigate crimes because she wanted to take the credit. She had her own reasons for wanting to solve Lakeside's mysteries and it had nothing to do with getting attention. So she decided to ask about the mayor instead, "So, Miles is up in arms, huh?"

"Oh, yeah, he's in a tizzy." Kip checked his watch, took his last swig of coffee, and then grabbed his remaining muffin. "Speaking of which, I should go. I'll see you tomorrow night?"

"Absolutely." She managed a smile while confirming their dinner date, but her thoughts were really still on the missing tiger case.

"Great!" He smiled back and turned for the door.

Janet Evans

Susan would have several more conversations that day, but only this one stayed on her mind. She was truly puzzled. *What would somebody do with a Bengal tiger? How would you even go about stealing a wild animal that weighs several hundred pounds?*

CHAPTER 2

Susan sat on the bench of her bay window next to her feline companion who was bathing in the late afternoon sun. She stroked his fur while trying to distract herself with plans for an upcoming retirement party she would be catering. But thoughts about work were overpowered by questions about the missing Bengal tiger, which had been swirling around her mind since that afternoon. At least now, she had someone to talk to about the case. "Mr. Giles, maybe you'll be interested in this new case. It's about a killer who abducted a cat."

Mr. Giles paused momentarily from his preening to look up at her as if he were indeed concerned about the missing feline and its murderous abductor.

"A Bengal tiger would have to weigh around 400 pounds, I would think. Even a well-trained tiger would put up a fight if he were being kidnapped, right? Then, how would you get him out of there without being noticed? You can't put him in your pocket. Wouldn't people get suspicious if you just drove a truck right up to the animal cages? It doesn't make sense."

Mr. Giles just purred, seemingly in agreement, and then continued his bath.

Susan pulled out her phone to see if she could find out more about the missing tiger. Fortunately for her, B & B circus' webpage was brimming with information about its prize white Bengal tiger, Zena. She was born in India 4 years ago in captivity. Zena had been with the circus for 2 years, weighed approximately 374 lbs and was roughly 8 feet long. If Zena were recovered she could easily be identified by what the website described as her "stripe pattern." Apparently, the stripes of the tiger are unique to each individual since it is caused by the pigmentation of the animal's skin. The stripe pattern would be visible even if the animal had been shaved. Also Susan learned that white tigers are white because of a genetic deficiency in pigmentation. After she had learned so much about Zena, she began to feel a personal connection. She wanted to know who had stolen this beautiful animal.

Susan waited for the heat of the late summer sun to stimulate her thoughts. But only one idea stubbornly persisted in her mind, she should go to the circus and investigate. Susan was less than enthused by this prospect. Her last visit to the circus had been when she was a little girl and it was one of the last memories she had of spending time with her father. The thought of attending the circus again flooded her mind with bittersweet memories. She had few precious moments of time alone with her father. He often seemed distant to her as a young girl, because he worked long hours in a job she did not understand at all. Unfortunately, he disappeared when she was four years old, before she had a chance to get to know him better. Susan was, above all, determined to find out what had happened to her father.

Susan and Kip actually bonded over mutual interest in unsolved savings and loan cases. Her father had been a loan officer who had gone missing in a major scandal in 1991, so her interest was personal. Kip had started off investigating savings and loans cases to improve his financial situation by uncovering some of the millions, maybe even billions, waiting to be discovered. He actually scored a few times already, which had served to keep his interest going. It had begun a few years ago as a modern day treasure hunt for him to apply his investigative skills. Eventually one of his investigations had put him on a collision course with Susan Becker. While investigating different angles of the 1991 scandal, they had discovered how closely aligned their interests were. Now they were both in it together for the long haul.

The problem was Kip's day job. Kip had taken the job as a small town detective thinking that it would leave him plenty of time for his side investigations into S & L cases. Much to his dismay, there had been something of a crime boom in the sleepy little town of Lakeside, MO. Most of his time had been diverted from his personal investigations into scandals from the 1990s toward the crimes of today which he had to investigate professionally. His partner, Frank Matthews, felt that Kip needed to focus on today's crimes and leave his "treasure hunting" to the past where it belonged. Susan, however, appreciated his help on her father's case and felt that they were making real headway. This was yet another reason why she wanted to help him close his other cases as soon as possible. As it turned out, Susan was actually quite the investigator in her own right, so she had been instrumental in closing several of his recent cases.

Deep down she wasn't driven by a love of mysteries, she just really hated open questions. Susan took a deep breath and reaffirmed her determination to solve this open question even if she did have to go to the circus to do it. She was convinced someone there had to know something. Maybe she and Mr. Giles might find a clue that the police had missed.

"Mr. Giles, do you want to go to the circus?" Susan inquired of her furry companion. Mr. Giles purred, gave her a sly kitty grin, then hopped down to the floor and walked toward the exit. He was halfway to the door when he shot an impatient glance in her direction. The look on his face was insistent, as if to say, "What are you waiting for? Let's go!"

CHAPTER 3

The scene at the red and white tent felt unpleasantly familiar for Susan. From kicking the gravel outside to the gentle crunch of the hay underfoot inside of the tent, it was all déjà vu. Her melancholy mood barred her from sharing the excitements of the rest of the audience although she could appreciate the performers were highly skilled and well rehearsed. Mr. Giles, on the other hand, seemed to thoroughly enjoy himself. He was especially enamored with the big cats in the first act, which included two lions and a remaining tiger. Susan paid rapt attention to this part as well, hoping to learn the faces of the performers who worked directly with the big cats and checking her program to learn their names. When intermission came, she pulled out some kitty treats for Mr. Giles, which he gulped down greedily.

Susan and Mr. Giles got up from the wooden risers; she hoped to find a snack for herself, and to get familiar with the grounds. She passed at least five vendors whose offerings she found undesirable, and then suddenly she stumbled over Mr. Giles who had suddenly stopped walking. There were large tracks on the ground leading outside of the main tent to a big black tent which was inaccessible from the customer parking lot. There were a few vehicles parked in a gravel lot between the animal's tent and a huge chain link fence, three large trucks were there with the B&B insignia prominently featured each of them.

Just then a booming voice rang out over the loudspeaker, "Ladies and gentleman, please return to your seats for the exciting second half of our show. Prepare to be amazed by the gravity defying feats of the Fantastic Flying Fentons."

Susan and Mr. Giles hurriedly returned to their seats to see the rest of the show. Mr. Giles was mesmerized by the acrobats and the trapeze artists who dominated the second act. She found his fascination to be disconcerting as she imagined the cat performing all manner of somersaults in her apartment. After the finale, Susan applauded loudly along with the rest of the audience even though her thoughts had remained far removed from the performance through the majority of the show. Getting into that black tent where the animals were held was her main focus. She hoped there would be an invitation to meet the animals after the final act, but no such invitation came. This would increase the level of difficulty of getting backstage. Additionally, Susan expected the security to be tight following the abduction of their prize white tiger, but to her surprise she accessed the performers' staging area without much ado. Only two middle-aged security stood between herself and the animal performers dwelling inside.

There were very few people tending to the animals inside the black tent. Susan scanned the faces for someone she had chosen for an interview. Bingo. Lenora the Great, the lion tamer from the performance, was talking to Lionel the lion in the corner opposite her. As she proceeded toward Lenora and Lionel, Susan noticed she had been collecting suspicious gazes from everyone in the room though they all continued to interact with the animals. As an outsider, her presence had not gone unnoticed even by the animals. Surely the same must have held true for the perpetrator, which meant someone here had to know something.

"You must be Lenora," Susan began. "My name is Susan Becker. I'm a friend of detective Kip Fletcher."

Lenora stared intently at Susan, while her thin face slowly bobbed up and down in a rhythmic motion. The look on the young, swarthy woman's face was one of curiosity. She was clearly sizing Susan up, deciding what to make of this interloper.

Susan smiled nervously. "Well, I heard about what happened last night. I just had some questions about the case, because I just don't understand how somebody could steal a tiger. I mean, how is that even possible?"

"So, you're a friend of Kip's, huh?" Lenora spoke with the distinctive accent of a New Englander. "You don't look like a cop." She observed plaintively, as though it made no difference to her one way or the other.

"Oh, I'm not," Susan replied. "I'm just…an interested third party. Would you mind answering a few questions? I can't seem to get this case off my mind."

"So you think you can find out who killed James?" Lenora responded.

"Maybe, I'm actually a pretty good investigator."

Lenora pondered this response momentarily, then shrugged, "What do you want to know?"

"Did you notice anyone strange around before this happened?"

"Yes, I sure did. I'll tell you the same thing I told the cops. A guy came around here a couple weeks before Zena was abducted. He claimed that he was a zoologist. And he could have been, you know? I mean, he talked the talk. He certainly knew a lot about Bengal tigers. He was no amateur. But...something was off, you know? Nothing he said, per se, but ... just a feeling that I had about him. I mean, he said he was interested in finding out about getting a Bengal tiger for the zoo where he worked, but his interest in Zena seemed more personal than professional. You know what I mean? "

"So you got a weird feeling from this guy? Did you catch his name?"

"No. I think he gave his name." She shook her head. "But I don't remember what it was. Kyle took a business card from the guy."

Kyle Brenner was Zena's trainer. Susan was very eager to speak with him. "Do you mean Kyle Brenner?

"Do you know him?"

"No, not exactly But I know of him and I'm a big fan. Is he here now?"

"I haven't seen him around much tonight," Lenora answered.

"Thanks a lot, Lenora, you have been really helpful."

Of course, Mr. Giles had long ago lost interest with the conversation between her and Lenora and wandered off. Susan was eager to find him before he managed to upset any of the trainers or animals. She tried calling his name, but Mr. Giles did not respond. Why would he? He was after all a cat, not a dog. As the minutes ticked by, the suspicious stares she had been receiving were taking a turn for the hostile, so she made her way toward the exit. Susan hoped that Mr. Giles would be waiting near her bike. When she reached her classic styled blue and white Schwinn, Mr. Giles was indeed resting comfortably in her basket. So she hopped on the banana seat and pondered the case while she pedaled home.

The trip was not altogether unproductive, but she hadn't learned as much as she'd hoped. She had intended to talk to Kyle and now there was this mysterious zoologist. Susan was having some trouble with her suspect list. There was no zoo in Lakeside, nor anywhere nearby, so she doubted that there were any zoo workers around here. There was probably a short list of locals with the capability to do this, maybe a veterinarian.

But as far as she knew, Dr. Peters was on his annual trip to Wales to visit his family. He had gone every year since she'd known him, so she never even tried to schedule an appointment for Mr. Giles during this time. Who was left? She needed information on the people of Lakeside: their work, their whereabouts, their visitors and maybe more.

The best source of information in Lakeside was Mrs. Caruthers. Fortunately for Susan, Lakeside is a small town and a chance encounter with Mrs. Caruthers would not be hard to arrange. She would ask her if anyone had zoo connections since she seemed to know everything about everybody.

When Susan arrived at her apartment, she noticed Mr. Giles had brought something with him. It was a screw that read Dibolt RU-6158 on it. Mr. Giles did love shiny things. It was obviously a custom part of something or other. She had no clue what use it might have. But he had given it to her, so she put it in her pocket and took it with her inside. Mr. Giles padded up the steps behind her. She knew he would not stand for her to throw away something he had collected. So she placed his treasure along with the others in his treasure case. He purred his approval, so she gave him a little pet, and then made her way straight for the shower.

CHAPTER 4

Kelly's Diner was owned by Kelly Jennings and was decorated in the classic diner style of a half century ago. The decor was black and white with deep crimson added for color. The tables, stools, and chair legs all gleamed in polished chrome. Kelly's menu also included classic diner fare, which rose above all competition. In addition, Kelly also had some tricks up her sleeve, such as a variety of specials created to showcase seasonal foods. Therefore, Kelly was not only a friend to local growers, but her diner was a favorite eatery for locals and tourists alike.

But Susan didn't come for the specials; she had come to Kelly's Diner because Kelly was Ellen Caruthers sister. Mrs. Caruthers was nothing, if not a creature of habit. She often ate dinner at her sister Kelly's diner. Susan made it a point to arrive at the diner a little after 5:45 hoping to bump into Mrs. Caruthers there. And since Susan had a dinner date with Kip this evening, she arranged to meet him at the diner forty-five minutes later. Susan found the two middle aged women chatting in a corner booth near the swinging doors that led to the kitchen. She approached them nonchalantly and sat in the booth across from the pair.

"Hello, Susan," Mrs. Caruthers greeted her. "How are you?"

"Oh, I'm just fine. Thank you, and yourself?"

"We're fine," Kelly answered for the both of them. "Would you like a drink? I'll get Cindy for you."

"No, I'm fine," Susan responded. "I'm actually waiting for someone. But I am glad that I ran into you, though. Do you happen to know if anyone here in town has ever worked at a zoo?"

"A zoo?" Kelly repeated, and then looked quizzically at her sister. "If someone worked at a zoo why would they want to live here? So far away, I mean."

"There is one person that springs to mind," Mrs. Caruthers began slowly. "David Marrin. He's a zookeeper or something like that. He went to high school here. You may have gone to school with him or one of his cousins, Allan and Rosa Dinkins?"

Susan nodded. "I had some classes with Allan. I vaguely remember a cousin."

Mrs. Caruthers continued, "He hasn't lived around here for awhile. He went out of state somewhere to college. He worked in a zoo, I think. Not in Missouri, though. You should probably ask Allan if you want any specifics. What's your interest?"

"Uh, I just have some questions about something in his expertise. "

"His expertise?" Mrs. Caruthers looked incredulous. The older woman's plump face jiggled with laughter. "The way I remember it, David's expertise was being a scoundrel. Poor Meg Dinkins did her best to raise him after his mother died, but that boy always had a scheme going. He gave his long suffering aunt and uncle all kinds of sleepless nights, I'm sure of that. I bet he couldn't wait to get out of Lakeside. And I'm not surprised he never came back, either. He was a square peg, that one."

"Really?" Susan wondered if Mrs. Caruthers might be wrong about David never returning to Lakeside. She was imagining a conversation with Allan about his cousin's recent whereabouts.

Mrs. Caruthers was ready to move on to another topic. Unfortunately for Susan, she was to be that new topic. "So, Miss Becker," her emphasis was clearly on the word Miss. This did not go unnoticed by either of the other women at the table. She winked at Kelly before continuing, "Miss Becker, when exactly do you intend to make an honest man out of that handsome detective Fletcher?"

Mrs. Caruthers eyebrows were raised, her eyes had taken on a prying tone, and her smile seemed innocent in a disproportional way. Susan felt distinctly uncomfortable sitting in the spotlight cast upon her by Mrs. Caruthers. Actually, both women sharing the table with Susan also appeared keenly interested in her response to this inquiry.

"Actually…Mrs. Caruthers," Susan paused briefly, "I prefer Ms." Susan put on a sweet and innocent smile. "I prefer Ms. Becker, thank you."

All three women laughed.

Then Susan turned her attention toward Kelly. "I think I would like that drink now."

Kelly smiled broadly, her eyes laughing. "Sure, hon, what would you like to have?"

"I would really love some of your peach iced tea, if you have it."

"Coming right up." Kelly hailed the waitress and ordered a round of iced teas for the table. The conversation from that point was light and non-invasive, but Susan was still relieved when Kip arrived to rescue her.

"It's been fun, ladies, but I have to go."

She met Kip by the door. They settled on a rectangular, red table by the window on the opposite side of the restaurant of Kelly's booth. A blonde-haired teenaged waiter appeared at their table promptly and offered drinks and menus. According to his nametag, he was Paul.

Susan and Kip both refused menus from their young waiter and started ordering immediately.

"Hi, Paul. I'd like a peach iced tea and a club sandwich," Susan requested.

"I'll have a coke and a Reuben sandwich," Kip followed quickly. "Thanks, Paul."

Paul jotted notes rapidly on his pad, thanked them with a nervous smile, and raced off to the kitchen.

"He must be new." Kip observed.

Susan wondered how much small talk would be necessary before she could start asking him about the tiger case. She decided to wait until their order came, so they would not be interrupted. They discussed a few innocuous topics such as the upcoming police department picnic. Susan began tapping her left foot in anticipation, the sole of her sneaker hit silently on the black and white tiled floor. Finally the food arrived.

As soon as the plates and cups were on the table, she asked in a falsely relaxed tone, "So have you learned anything about the missing tiger case?"

Kip chuckled while dipping his fries in the extra Russian dressing that came with his sandwich. "How long have you been waiting to ask me that?"

"Since you arrived," she admitted.

They both laughed.

"Well, we have two possible suspects. There's Kyle Brenner, the tiger's trainer. You always have to assume that it could be an inside job in a case like this one."

"That makes sense. You said there's another suspect?"

"Yes and no. Brenner told us a story about a zoologist who he claims was sniffing around for the tiger recently. He gave us a business card for the guy. The name on the card, of course, was for a person who doesn't exist. The good news is that it was one of those slick coating business cards and we were able to pull some prints off the card. The bad news is that they don't match any in the system. So we're nowhere with identifying that individual. Anyway, the story could be bogus. Lately, Kyle has been reluctant to answer questions and he's been making himself scarce, so he's my chief suspect right now."

"But didn't Lenora corroborate his story? "

Kip cocked his head to the side. "How do you know Lenora?" It was more accusation than question.

"I may have attended a recent performance of B & B circus."

"Is that right? You went to my crime scene and questioned a potential witness? Do you understand that the people who committed this crime could find out that you are working this case? This is not a good idea. You do not have the badge to protect you. Whoever committed this crime is likely to be a very dangerous individual. They managed to subdue and abduct a tiger! Do you have any idea what they will do with you if they find you snooping around trying to incriminate them?"

Kip's eyes bored into hers. She squirmed under his gaze, but she was not planning to make any excuses. "I was in a public place enjoying an evening out with Mr. Giles. There's no law against that."

"I can see I'm wasting my breath," he muttered. "But you may as well know that Lenora is Kyle's sister. She would lie for him."

Regardless of what Kip said, Lenora appeared to Susan to be telling the truth. If she was lying she was certainly very good at it.

"The other suspect we have is this mystery zoo worker. We figure if this Kyle is telling the truth, then the other guy is a suspect. We have a piece of a glove with some blood on it, but nothing yet from that. We sent it to Springfield in hopes that it could be our first real piece of useful evidence."

"What do you know about cause of death for James?"

"Mr. Dennison's cause of death is undetermined. He was injected with something, which we can't pin down. We're also hoping to get some results back from the tox screen in Springfield. All we have for him right now is time of death. Maybe tomorrow."

CHAPTER 5

Allan Dinkins was behind the counter at Main Street Pharmacy when Susan walked in. He was practically barricaded in behind a half wall of candy bars, snacks, thermometers and a myriad of other products which were strategically placed to entice the customer into making an extra purchase before checking out. It was almost quitting time for Allan and he was fidgeting impatiently with his eyes glued to the clock on his register which read 7:42. "Come on 8 o'clock," he murmured under his breath.

Susan walked up to the counter. "Hey, Allan."

"Hiya, Sue, how's it going?" He seemed relieved for the distraction. She had guessed from the near empty parking lot outside that it had been a slow night.

"Pretty good. But you know I bought some Double Stuff Oreos here last week that looked like they only had one and a half times the stuff. Is there anything you can do about that?"

"I'll look into it, "Allan smiled. Susan could have talked to him about anything, he was glad for any diversion. "Is there anything I can help you find?"

"No but actually there is someone you can help me find. I've been researching exotic animals for a personal project I'm working on. And I remembered that your cousin worked for a zoo. Was his name David?"

"Yeah, his name was David. He's dead. "

"David's dead? What happened?"

"Yeah, last month in a house fire."

"Wow, that's unfortunate."

Allan shrugged. "I guess, but I never thought he'd live till old age."

"Really? Why's that?"

"Dave was the kind of guy that knew how to make enemies. He always had some scheme going. He owed everybody money, including me. If he hadn't died in the fire, I would've sworn that he it was an insurance scam. That's right up Dave's alley. He was in debt up to his eyeballs. Student loans, upside down mortgage, you name it."

"Did you go to the funeral?"

"Me?" he asked incredulously. "Nah, we weren't that close. Why should I drive all the way to Cincinnati to watch him get put in the ground? My family went."

"Rosa, too?"

"Yeah, Rosa and David always got along well. She went along with him on some of his schemes." Allan looked at his register. "It's time for me to cash out." He announced, pushed a sequence of buttons resulting in the cash drawer popping out. He removed the black drawer from its place and set it on the shelf underneath the main counter before looking up at Susan. "Are you asking about Dave because you think he stole that tiger?"

"Honestly, I did think that at first."

"Well, if he was still around, I'd be tempted to agree with you. He's certainly worked with a lot of animals."

"Thanks, Allan, for satisfying my curiosity. I should go. It looks like you've got to close up soon."

"Yeah, actually I do. I really need to concentrate when I count out my drawer."

"No problem, I'll talk to you later."

"Sure thing," he responded, and then his attention returned quickly to the cash he was counting.

She had left Mr. Giles waiting outside in the basket of her bicycle. When she emerged from the pharmacy, though, he was gone. This whole trip had been a disaster. She was almost positive she had a potential suspect in David Marrin. Now that lead was gone. And to top it off, she was going to have to go hunt down Mr. Giles. She walked along the pharmacy wall to where her bike was chained to a lamppost, hoping that he might be close by, see her, and return. No such luck.

Where had that crazy cat gotten off to now?

Susan walked east toward the nearest park, hoping to find some signs of where Mr. Giles may have gone. Just when she was about to give up and let Mr. Giles meet her at home, she saw the old fairgrounds. It looked like the kind of place with plenty of places for a cat to play or hide. She saw Mr. Giles off in the distance but he made no moves toward her. After testing the fence extensively for possible entry points, she finally found a weak spot in the chain link fence that allowed her to easily access the expansive fair grounds.

She walked past the abandoned ticket booth toward an old rickety, faded blue tent, which announced the town's Bi-Centennial anniversary. She believed this was close to where she had seen Mr. Giles. He poked his body out of the tent without fully emerging from it. Susan noticed he had hay in his fur, the hay was not a surprise, but that the hay appeared fresh was an anachronism. What was fresh hay doing here?

It wasn't yet dark outside, but the natural light was fading fast and it would be nonexistent from the interior of the tent. Great! In the fading sunlight she fumbled around in her purse until she retrieved her cell phone. A holster would be a much more convenient place to put her phone, she wished she had one. Her phone's flashlight app helped her immensely in her efforts to locate her wayward cat. After a few steps inside Mr. Giles joined her.

Up to this point in her investigation, she had been fixated on identifying suspects. She wondered why it had never occurred to her to consider where in town someone might keep a tiger. Obviously her suspect and the missing tiger had been here recently. Some of the signs of Zena's presence were smellier than others she noticed as she stepped in an unpleasant remnant of the tiger's occupancy. Eww! She became engaged in a futile effort to clean off her shoes with the hay.

She doubted the perpetrator had taken the tiger out on the town. Whoever had been keeping Zena here was probably not coming back. It was likely that Zena was gone for good.

Susan continued walking around the tent and came across nothing that appeared to be a promising clue. She decided that she had better call Kip. He answered on the first ring. She shared the story of the evening's events with him.

"I'm on my way." He sounded fatigued. "Hey, Suzie, I'm going to tell Frank that I got an anonymous tip. Your best bet is to get out of there before we arrive."

"Sounds good. I can't wait to get out of here and get cleaned up."

CHAPTER 6

Susan struggled to open a new bag of Kitty Delights, which was predictably difficult to accomplish. She always wondered what these bags were really designed to protect, certainly cat food did not require such secure packaging. Mr. Giles growing impatience was not helping the situation any, so she abandoned her efforts to open the bag with her bare hands and sought out her scissors. Finally, she was dumping the dry cat food into the blue ceramic bowl. Once that step was complete, she washed her hands in the bathroom and completed her mental plans for this evening's dinner with Kip. She was expecting him to arrive any minute with the main course for this evening's meal.

Just then she heard a knock on her door. She opened it to find Kip with two bags of food. And unless her nose was deceiving her, one of the bags contained barbecue ribs. They shared a brief hug as she invited him in.

"Tonight I'm making dinner," Kip announced.

"Really? That sounds great," she agreed without hesitation.

Kip walked directly into the kitchen. He set the bags down on the island. Out of one, he pulled out a full rack of ribs, sautéed mixed veggies, and a container of macaroni and cheese. Out of the other bag emerged all of the fixings for a beautiful broccoli salad. He had whipped up the salad while warming the ribs and macaroni up in her oven. Dinner was ready and on her kitchen table in less than twenty minutes.

"Thanks, Kip. This dinner really looks really great."

Looks were not deceiving. The food was excellent. Hearty, comfort food was the perfect way to end her day as they discussed a variety of topics.

"Do you want to watch a movie?" Kip suggested.

"Did you find out anything new about the tiger case?"

"First of all, I've said this before but obviously it's worth repeating. What you did last night could have been very dangerous. I know that Mr. Giles wanders off and that you needed to look for him. I get that. But as soon as you realize that you are standing in a crime scene, then you should leave. Immediately. You do realize that the murderer could have shown up at any minute, don't you?"

"I understand." She managed to pacify him, while making sure not to agree to anything. She was a grown woman who did not take orders; surely Kip knew that by now.

"We dusted the chains and collar, they've got Kyle Brenner's prints on them, but he was the tiger's trainer. And we found a cell phone with some unidentified prints."

"Are you going to arrest him?"

Kip gave her that charming smile he often gave when he was about to withhold information. "You know I can't tell you that."

Susan realized that she probably wouldn't get any more information just by asking. So she decided to switch gears by giving him some information. "It was easy enough for me to slip through the fence, but I wasn't transporting a tiger. I would think you would need a large vehicle for that and some way to get in through the locked gates. You'd have to have some help. Some local help preferably."

"Frank and I thought of that, we're looking at the groundskeepers to shed some light. The supervisor gave us a list of names."

"So who's the supervisor? If you don't mind my asking." She added the last part in an attempt at cordiality.

"Rosa Dinkins."

"You're kidding."

"No." He paused and looked at her knowingly. "Susan, there's something you are not telling me."

"It could just be a coincidence."

"Spill it."

"The other day when I was at the circus with Mr. Giles."

He gave her a disapproving look.

"It's a free country, I'm allowed to go out to a circus if I want to, aren't I? And for your information Mr. Giles happens to enjoy the circus."

"Go on," he said in a voice that let her know he was not at all convinced by that explanation, but he was more interested at present in the ends of her unlawful investigation than the means.

"Anyway, I was talking to Lenora and she said there was a zoologist who came by to talk to them about getting a white tiger for his zoo. She said the guy was acting really suspicious."

Kip nodded. It didn't seem to be the first time he had heard this story.

"Well, I thought of David Marrin. He was a guy who used to live around here. I knew he worked at a zoo. I thought maybe it was him. "

"And?" Kip's voice was bordering on excitement.

"And Rosa Dinkins is David's cousin."

Kip was clearly pleased. "Well, we might have a couple of suspects here."

"Wait. There's something you should know. I already talked to Allan Dinkins, Rosa's brother, and found out that David is dead."

"What? When?"

"Last month."

Kip was obviously deflated by this news. "Well, that's the best alibi I ever heard."

"But that's a pretty big coincidence, though, don't you think?"

Kip sighed. "No, not really. This David guy only came to your mind because he's from here. This prior incident in question happened before they came to Lakeside. So the guy who was asking about this tiger may not be from around here. If that happened at all, it could be just a story this trainer came up with to throw us off the trail. Besides, Susan, there is one thing I know for sure about the perpetrator of this crime. And that is that he, or she, is definitely alive. "

It's still a big coincidence. Susan thought she'd stop by Rosa's house and see if she knew anything.

"Do you want to watch TV? "

Susan handed Kip the remote for him to choose a program. He wandered aimlessly through the channels for something they would both enjoy. He found a show entitled "Nature" on PBS. According to the description, it was about tigers. Kip smiled conspiratorially and selected the program. When he turned the channel on there was a narrator discussing Bengal tigers in their natural environment.

He laughed. "Sometimes, a coincidence is just a coincidence. "

Susan snuggled with Kip on the couch until the nature program ended.

"Would you like some dessert?" Susan asked.

"Sure!"

Susan hopped off the couch and started toward the kitchen. "I've got some brownies here, some toppings, and some ice cream"

"Yes to all of that." Kip hopped off the couch and practically raced her to the kitchen.

Shortly thereafter they were side by side in the kitchen, preparing individual brownie sundaes. Susan warmed her brownie briefly in the microwave before topping it with whipped cream, pecans, and chocolate chips. Two scoops of vanilla ice cream and hot fudge sauce finished it off. Kip topped his brownie with pretzels and chocolate covered mixed nuts.

Then he finished it just as she had, with two scoops of vanilla ice cream and hot fudge sauce.

"I don't know how you can eat that," she always questioned his affinity for salty foods mixed with sweet ones. "Pretzels in a sundae?"

"Just watch me and I'll show you." He took a huge bite of his dessert. "You see, it's not hard at all, you just open your mouth and chew."

She just shook her head at him. "You're being silly."

They walked over to her bay window and sat across from each other in the bench seat to watch the stars together. Their sundaes were consumed in a contented silence. Each enjoyed their own dessert creation, as well as the pleasure of each other's company, immensely. As soon as they had finished eating, Kip nudged Susan's feet until she giggled. It was obvious by the amused look on his face that he was planning to continue testing her levels of ticklishness. Mr. Giles, obviously feeling that he had been neglected so far this evening, jumped up on the bench between them. He purred contentedly when Susan stroked his fur, and then she allowed him to settle himself on her lap.

Finally, Kip broke the silence, "I have to get up early. I should really go."

Susan stood to walk with him to the back door, which led to a wooden staircase outside. At the doorway, she contemplated whether she should give him a kiss goodnight. Before she had made up her mind, he pulled her close and kissed her softly on the lips. Instead of lingering there, he simply pulled back and whispered directly into her ear, "Good night."

He was down the steps before she had a chance to second guess their last brief encounter. "Good night," she said to no one in particular, and then pushed the door closed on the evening.

CHAPTER 7

Meghan and Kenton Dinkins had taken their retirement money across the border to Mexico, where they had purchased a beautiful seaside property. Susan remembered they had shown the pictures to everyone who crossed their path. The younger Dinkins, Allan and Rosa, had lived together in their childhood home for less than a year. Now Rosa lived in the split-level home alone. Susan rode down Garner Street searching for anything that looked familiar; unfortunately there was nothing distinctive about the house she sought. Most of the homes in this neighborhood were built in the 1950's with only five basic floor plans, yielding several identical houses with nothing to distinguish between them besides the color. The house she was looking for was blue, she reminded herself. It was definitely 1100 and something. Susan had foolishly relied on her fragile memory, even though she had not visited the Dinkins' house since she went to Allan's 5th grade graduation party when she was 10. How was she supposed to find the place again after all these years? Eventually she spotted a house that she thought might be it. Susan hoped that Rosa would answer the bell to confirm. Instead an elderly woman with flawless skin that resembled a caramel macchiato appeared.

"Can I help you, hon?" she inquired of Susan.

"Mrs. Perkins! It's so nice to see you again." She hadn't seen much of her 3rd grade teacher recently and it really was a pleasant surprise.

"Susan, I've been meaning to come into your shop, but I've been really busy this summer. What brings you by?"

"I was actually looking for Rosa Dinkins."

"Well, I'm afraid you're on the wrong street. The Dinkins live on Garner Court. Same house number. 1174 Garner Court."

"I'm sorry, Mrs. Perkins, it really looks the same and the address is similar."

"Don't worry about it, Sue. It's good to see you. Besides, this kind of thing happens all the time. Sometimes I even get their mail." Mrs. Perkins chuckled good-naturedly. "Speaking of which, I was just looking at my mail and found some of Rosa's stuff mixed in. Since you're going by there anyway, would you mind dropping it off?"

"No problem." Susan waited patiently for the older woman to return.

Armed with the correct address, she arrived quickly to her destination. Susan stood at the Dinkins' doorstep with a package of pastries in hand. Susan rang the doorbell, hoping that Rosa would be at home. After she rang twice and was about to leave, the young brunette appeared in an old St Louis

Rams t-shirt and a pair of faded blue jeans. Rosa greeted Susan with a puzzled expression.

"Hi, Susan, how are you?"

"I'm fine, thanks. I actually came by to see how you were doing. Allan told me about what happened to David. I know he was like a brother to you. I just wanted to express my condolences. I'm very sorry for your loss."

Rosa's face brightened. "Thanks, Susan, I really appreciate that." She smiled when Susan presented the box of baked treats. "And what's this?"

"Just some pastries, I thought you might like. I brought a few doughnuts and cookies to sweeten up your day a little bit. I hope you like them."

"Oh, I'm sure I will. Would you like to come in? Have a treat and a cup of coffee."

"Sure. Can I bring Mr. Giles? I'm sure he'll appreciate the company of another cat."

"Yeah, he can come play with Jingles."

"That would be great." Susan pulled Mr. Giles out of the basket, and then followed Rosa into the house while carrying him in her arms. Susan entered into the split-level home and looked around for anything that seemed to be amiss. No dice.

The only thing she noticed was that Rosa wasn't much for decorating. The place looked just the way she remembered it. Even the same polka dot couch was in the living room. Susan only remembered that because it was the only polka dot couch she'd ever seen anywhere.

"Well, Jingles is definitely around here somewhere." Rosa must have assumed that Susan was looking around for Jingles. "He's probably in the backyard hunting under the deck. He's very territorial; he doesn't like anyone on his turf." Rosa gestured toward the glass doors that led out to her deck. Susan took the hint and walked over to the glass doors, opened them, then released Mr. Giles. He spotted Jingles immediately and bounded off in the direction of the other cat.

Meanwhile, the air began to fill up with the comforting aroma of freshly brewed coffee. Susan strategically chose a seat at Rosa's round kitchen table, where she would be in the best position to take a panoramic view of her environment. With her back to the wall, she was able to see the backyard through the patio windows on her right, keep an eye on Rosa in the kitchen, and still see through the open doorway to the living room on her left.

"My dad always taught us to never throw anything out if you still have a use for it," Rosa stated as she pulled coffee creamer out of the refrigerator. "I remind myself of that every time I open up this hideous avocado green fridge." Rosa deposited the creamer onto the kitchen table next to a small tray of coffee fixings, which obviously saw frequent use. Then she headed for the pantry in the corner on the opposite side of the room.

Susan chuckled at the green fridge that didn't seem to match anything else in the kitchen. Secretly, she was happy to hear that Rosa was not in the habit o discarding things. If she had taken her father's training to heart, maybe she had held onto some evidence.

"Before I forget, I have some of your mail." Susan pulled the envelopes out of her purse and noticed that Rosa had stopped rummaging through the pantry.

"I should explain that," Susan added quickly. "What I meant is that I was on my way here, I got turned around, ended up at your neighbor's house and she gave me some mail for you."

"Mrs. Perkins," Rosa murmured absentmindedly into the pantry as she pulled out a package of biscotti. She closed the door. "That happens all the time. Thanks for bringing it by. Could you just leave it on that desk in the corner?" Susan walked over to the desk in the corner and saw several envelopes there, mostly bills. She set the new mail next to the old and noticed an unopened box there that caught her eye. It had the name Dibolt on the top, she looked back to see if Rosa was watching. Susan picked the box up to look for additional information. On the side of the box were the words "Model Number: RU-6158."

Susan swiveled around quickly to return to the table. If she stayed any longer, she was sure to attract unwanted attention from her hostess.

When she returned to the table, Susan continued to look around for anything suspicious. But there was nothing. She looked outside in the backyard. Nothing. Finally after about fifteen minutes of chitchat, Susan excused herself to go to the bathroom. While in the bathroom, she shuffled through the medicine cabinet to no avail. Then she saw a vial of something in the toilet tank. What was this? Obviously, they didn't want anyone to see it. She couldn't take it with her, but she didn't want to get caught snooping in Rosa's bathroom.

I'll take a picture of it! Susan reached into her pocket and pulled out her phone. She couldn't pronounce the name of this medicine and she had no idea what use it might have. But it could be a clue, so she snapped a shot of the vial from every angle.

Susan rushed back to the kitchen, hoping not to arouse the suspicion of her hostess, and sat down for some friendly chitchat with Rosa. Shortly thereafter both of the women finished their coffee, and then went into the backyard to check on the cats. Mr. Giles and Jingles were playing underneath the deck.

"We should really get going," Susan stated. "Thanks so much, Rosa, for having us over."

Rosa responded, "Sure, no problem. Thank you for the pastries."

"Sorry again about David."

"Yeah, me too."

Susan hopped on her bike with Mr. Giles in the basket. She was passing the library on the way home, so she decided to stop off to get on the Internet to further her investigation into the clues she had found. There were a variety of industrial tools at the Dibolt website, so she added RU-6158 into the internal search. The search turned up a bolt cutter, so she printed the page to check it against the screw she had at her home. But she was certain this was a match and that Rosa was somehow involved. Now to find out more about this medicine she had discovered— Tenazol. Susan was disappointed with the results of that search. Though it was listed for use as a tranquilizer for wild animals, it could also be used as a tranquilizer for household pets. Maybe Rosa was just hiding the medicine from Jingles. If she had a sedative in the house for Mr. Giles, she would certainly want to hide it. Maybe this wasn't a clue. But something else on the package was worthy of investigation. Who was this Dr. M.I. Zimmerman? She searched for him on the Internet and found out that he was a veterinarian based in White Plains, NY. The business address of record for B&B circus was also in White Plains. Now that was definitely more than a coincidence.

CHAPTER 8

Susan was stocking her doughnut racks when Kip showed up for breakfast. Susan had been waiting rather anxiously for him to arrive. Kip sat at on the cream-colored vinyl stool across the counter from her. "Do you have any sour cream doughnuts today? You know how much I love those."

His smirk let her know that he was interested in an update on the case and that he was in no rush to discuss it. She enjoyed this dance, maybe he would give her something if she gave him something first, "Sure, have one on the house."She offered him a warm sour cream doughnut on a napkin.

"Don't mind if I do." He ate the doughnut slowly and deliberately in total silence.

"Kip, tell me!" she insisted impatiently. "Did you find any new clues?"

"Rosa, the groundskeeper didn't have an alibi, so Frank and I paid her a visit and imagine my surprise when I saw a box of pastries from your bakery sitting on her kitchen counter. Now that is my idea of a coincidence!"

"My bakery is very popular."

"So you are saying that you didn't go to her house to investigate?

"No, I'm not saying that. Mr. Giles and I paid a friendly visit to a grieving neighbor. That's not illegal, the last time I checked."

"Well, it doesn't matter anyway. We have a more viable suspect now. "

"We received an anonymous tip that Kyle Brenner was spotted at the old fairgrounds tent where Zena was being held. We pulled up and there he was. We feel like he was there to find something he left behind. So we picked him up. We got a warrant and found plenty of goodies back at his trailer. He's down at the station now."

"Has he confessed? "

"Nope. He hasn't said anything useful at all. Now his lawyer has advised him to exercise his right to remain silent, which is a shame, because our case is pretty weak as of now. It would be nice if he could fill in the gaps for us," Kip said jokingly. "His prints were on the chain and the collar, but that is something any good defense attorney will explain away. But some of the evidence we found at his place is a horse of another color. All in all, there are still pieces missing from this puzzle."

Susan strongly agreed with that assessment of the situation. "So has he told you anything about why he was there?

"Oh, sure, before he went silent, Kyle says he received a ransom note for Zena's safe return. He was supposed to meet the kidnapper at the old fairgrounds."

"Really? Did he have any proof of that? "

"Not really."

"Do you think he did it?" Susan wondered aloud.

"Well, it comes down to motive, means, and opportunity. He's got opportunity. That's the beauty of an inside job, he's got unlimited access. A white tiger is worth a fortune to some unsavory types, so he's got motive. It's the means that I'm still working on. What kind of connections does he have here in Lakeside? Specifically, how did he end up taking the tiger to the old fairgrounds? Maybe conspirators are what I'm looking for now." Kip shook his head. "Honestly, Suzy, something is off in this case. I'd certainly be open to other suspects if I had any."

"What about Rosa?"

"Oh, she's still on the suspect list, she's just not a frontrunner right now. "

Kip's phone rang. "Fletcher," he answered. Then Kip turned his back to put some distance between them, making it more difficult for Susan to eavesdrop. But she still followed along on his end.

"You found it?"

"Where?"

"A match?"

"Uh, huh"

"Really? It's not the perp's?"

"Great!"

"See you soon."

It was easy to surmise that Kip was not planning to share whatever enlightenment he had received about the case. Maybe she could charm it out of him.

"So, Kip, would you like to wash down that doughnut with a cup of coffee? "

"No, thanks, Suzie. Frank's waiting for me. I'll see you later, alright?"

And just like that he was heading toward the parking lot. From Susan's viewpoint this was an unsatisfactory end to their interchange, which would not be left unsettled. Susan couldn't get his conversation off her mind; the questions swam through her mind, so she had to know what was new with the case. Julie Hanson, her high school helper, would be here this afternoon that would give her the opportunity to act on the plan she was formulating in her mind. If she brought Kip lunch at the station, she would be in a position to absorb some new information about the case.

The Miller County Sheriff's department was housed in the type of non-descript muddy brown brick building that was reserved for local government. Susan chained her bike to the flagpole outside as the Missouri state flag waved in the breeze above. She grabbed the bag of food from her basket and hurried up the cement steps and in through the glass doors. Her goal was to catch Kip by surprise, so she was hoping to get to his desk without anyone alerting him of her presence. The first obstacle to overcome would be the receptionist, Marcy. Armed with a few gingerbread cookies and a plausible story, Susan entered the glass doors into the foyer. Fortunately, the receptionist desk had been vacated, Marcy was probably at lunch. Perfect timing, Susan thought to herself as she slipped undetected into the room where Kip's desk sat, also empty. Casually, she took notice of the files on his desk; none seemed to directly pertain to the tiger case. Her first reaction was disappointment, but then a second thought emerged. Kip was here, his computer was on a logout screen, and if he had left his computer would be off according to department regulations. So if the file wasn't here, maybe he was working on the case right now, he could be interviewing a suspect. To validate her suspicions went to locate Detective Fletcher. Creeping quietly past the Interrogation room, she heard his familiar voice leaked through the closed wooden door into the hallway She was delighted to find him there just as she had hoped. Susan's eyes darted around for a place to eavesdrop without being noticed. As soon as she found one she listened intently to the conversation.

"....the ransom note was just a ploy to get him out of his place and give the real perpetrators time to plant evidence there." Susan thought Kip must be talking about Kyle Brenner.

The response came quickly from another familiar voice, Frank Matthews, whose tone was dismissive "Those are the facts according to Brenner."

"Well, somebody believes him. B & B paid his bail."

"Lenora personally bailed him out. She's been backing his story from the beginning. But she is his sister, so the fact that she believes him, doesn't mean much of anything in my book."

"Honestly, I'm not sure he did it. First, he has a story of some mystery zookeeper. Then this new ransom note story. You and I know that sometimes, truth is stranger than fiction. Think about that grave robbing case with the missing corpse. Kyle's story is almost too crazy to be a lie. And he seemed genuinely upset when we told him that his tiger may be gone for good."

"Why am I not surprised?" Frank Matthews was not a man for sentiment. "Every shred of evidence we have points directly at this man. If you ask me, the guy is as guilty as sin. The fact that he keeps coming up with one cockamamie story after another is far from compelling. I think the true story is that he kidnapped his own tiger and then sold it on the black market. Then I think our boy realized that he knows a lot more about training tigers than he does about committing crimes. He's in over his head, now he's looking for a way out. This happens all the time."

"Yeah, and that's another thing. Every shred of evidence points to him. Even if he's not a career criminal, he's probably not an idiot. Who leaves that much evidence lying around? We have the glove with the tiger's blood all over it. Not to mention, the bolt cutters in his trailer. He just leaves it there in plain sight for the cops to find? It doesn't make any sense why he wouldn't just get rid of that stuff!"

"Hey, if you have a better theory, I am willing to discuss it."

"I think it's possible that it happened exactly the way he said it did. Think about it. The real perp figures that we're getting too close. He needs a fall guy, so he decides to frame Kyle. First contact he makes with him, he gives him a phony story and a bogus business card. Now the perp does this knowing full well that no one is going to believe him when he tells this story. Then after the perp commits the crime, he sends Kyle a ransom note. Why? To plant evidence. He knows that Kyle will be out, so he can leave a bunch of clues at his place. It's actually not a bad plan. Kyle tells his story, proclaims his innocence, nobody listens, Brenner goes to prison and the real perpetrator lives out his days in luxury."

"That is not a bad plan," Frank repeated thoughtfully. "But framed by who? Do we have any other suspects?"

"The mystery zookeeper?

"He's a ghost, a figment of our perp's imagination."

"What about Lenora? She corroborated that part of the story."

"Now there's a co-conspirator if I ever saw one. We've been saying all along that he must be working with someone."

"I think we have to talk to this Rosa Dinkins, maybe we'll get a new name."

"I think a bird in the hand is worth two in the bush."

"That's because you've got no imagination"

"Fortunately for me, I don't need an imagination. I don't write children's books, I'm a detective."

Both of the men laughed good-naturedly. The tension in the previous conversation was gone when they began talking again.

"Do we have any matches for our unidentified prints from the SIM card or the business card?"

"Not necessarily. But it wasn't a total dead end. Tentatively, our techs believe that we have a match for the prints on both pieces of evidence. Of course, we can't be sure until we have someone to print. But we can work under the assumption that both sets of prints came from the same person."

"Well, we always knew he had a partner. So we're back to Rosa? She knows more than she's telling us. "

"Do we have enough for an arrest warrant? "

"I doubt it. She doesn't have an alibi, but that's not a crime. Neither is losing your cell phone at work. And this possible match of fingerprints for an as yet unidentified third party is not likely to impress anyone."

"Let's get something to eat," Frank suggested.

Susan's eyes darted up and down the hallway for a way to escape before the two men emerged. She was certain she'd be spotted if she headed back toward Kip's desk, because there was an officer standing right by the entrance to the hallway. She was leaning against the wall engrossed in a file. Susan reviewed her options quickly and headed away from Kip's desk. The bathroom door was ajar and she slipped in without attracting attention.

Susan washed her hands in the bathroom and thought about the case. How did these new pieces fit into the puzzle? The blood was Zena's and they found part of the glove at the crime scene and the other part in Kyle's place. He also had the bolt cutters. Rosa is definitely involved in some way and maybe Lenora, too.

Kip was standing over his desk with her lunch bag in his hand and a puzzled expression on his face.

"Hi, Kip, I was thinking about you and I thought I'd surprise you with lunch."

"Where did you just come from?" he asked, noticing that she had approached his desk from the opposite direction of the entrance.

"Uh, I just got here a little while ago, but I had to use the bathroom. So I left the food on your desk until I got back."

They shared a tasty lunch of chicken salad sandwiches, fruit, potato chips, and sodas.

"I love your chicken salad, Suzie, what's your secret?" asked Kip.

"I add bacon, green onions, and extra sharp cheddar cheese."

 "Well, it's pretty amazing!"

"Thanks. So how's the case?"

"I was wondering when you were going to ask me that. " He smirked. "Nothing's happening with the case. We got nothing new."

"Well, I may have something new for you. I wondered if you found any Dibolt bolt cutters in the course of your investigation."

"Yes, actually I have." Kip put his sandwich down, and then leaned across the desk. Obviously he was interested in this topic "I found them at our suspect's place. Why do you ask?"

"Mr. Giles found a part from some Dibolt bolt cutters in the tent at the old fairgrounds, the part was broken. I have it at my house. Interestingly, I also saw a replacement part for Dibolt bolt cutters at Rosa's house."

"Well, that is interesting." Kip had his notepad in his hand and his pen was waiting. "What else do you have?"

"She had a sedative in her house, one that could've been used to sedate Zena. I have a picture that you might want to see. "

Kip took a long while examining the picture and jotting down some additional notes. "Well, this is interesting. What do you know about this stuff?"

"It's a prescription strength sedative, prescribed by a Dr. Maury Zimmerman. He works in White Plains, NY. And as you know, B & B circus is also based in White Plains. It seems like she must be working with someone on the inside."

"This is beautiful." Kip covered his face with his hands, and then gave a disgusted sigh. He ran his palm the entire length of his face before speaking. "How am I supposed to introduce this evidence? Where could I have obtained this picture? If I use the anonymous tip card again, Judge Turner is going to think that I am framing these suspects myself. If this evidence had been obtained legally, I would have enough to get an arrest warrant for Rosa. I could flip her and find out who the inside man is. But I can't take this to a judge. I know she is involved, but I can't arrest her."

"Kip..." the look on his face made her unsure whether or not she should finish the statement. "I was just trying to help..." Her voice trailed off.

"It's not your fault, Susan, I just....I'm just not hungry right now. " Kip snapped the plastic seals back onto the containers left out on his desk. "I should really get back to work. I have to figure out a legal way to tie this all together." His voice was kind, but his eyes betrayed his exasperation. Susan packed up silently and left the building without a word. As Susan got on her bicycle, she decided that she and Mr. Giles needed to pay another visit to the Dinkins' home.

CHAPTER 9

Susan still had a theory to test and she knew she could act on it more swiftly than the police. Susan parked her bike under a streetlight on Garner Street less than a block away from the Dinkins' home. Without making eye contact with anyone, she moved quickly and purposefully until she was finally across the neatly trimmed lawn from Rosa's house. Trying hard not to attract attention, she sneaked across the lawn to the left hand side of the house. She was completely still for several minutes, laying flush against the blue siding waiting to see if anyone had noticed her. Mr. Giles found this clandestine task to be second nature, he turned the corner. When Susan was certain she had gone unnoticed, she looked for Mr. Giles. He was taking a particular interest in a patch of moss that appeared to be loose, scratching it persistently, paying no attention to her presence. Susan returned to her previous place to look for anything that might incriminate Rosa.

Mr. Giles suddenly appeared right next to her, with a small patch of moss in his claws. Susan tried to return to her search of the perimeter, but Mr. Giles refused to be ignored. He entangled himself in her feet when she tried to turn away. Susan had no idea why he was so focused on this moss, but she figured the best thing to do to appease him was to take a look. He had uncovered what looked like a shiny new latch or a lock of some kind. Further investigation revealed a door underneath the area where the moss had been.

Susan was in no rush to enter through this door. First, she wanted to have an idea of what she was getting herself into. Because no windows were visible below the house, it didn't appear to be a basement. Bomb shelters were popular during the cold war, but it could just be an ordinary cellar down there. But claustrophobia wasn't what gave her pause. She was concerned that there may be a Bengal tiger lurking around down there or, even worse, Rosa's accomplice.

Convinced finally to open the wooden door, only a dark hole awaited her. The flashlight app on her phone lit up an exceedingly uninviting tight, confined, and dark space. She saw what appeared to be a small cellar which could be accessed only through this crawlspace. Not quite ready to proceed, she measured the space with her eyes to see if it were large enough to fit an adult tiger. Mr. Giles, however, was feeling no trepidation. He hopped into the dark hole and quickly disappeared from view. Susan returned to her snooping, but stopped dead when she heard leaves rustling in the wooded area behind the backyard. Around the corner she found the spot where she was least likely to be seen, her eyes were trained on the woods looking for any movement. After what felt like an eternity, the shadowy outline of a man slowly emerged from the woods.

The man was at a distance, so Susan could not be sure who it was. As he came closer, she thought he looked familiar. He was older, more muscular, and his hair was different than she remembered. This man looked like David Marrin! Of course, that wasn't possible, w as it? While she was contemplating the possibilities, she couldn't help but notice that he was quickly approaching the area where she was standing. Between the house and the bushes was the perfect place to hide. If this guy was David Marrin, then she had been correct in suspecting him in the first place.

Susan was delighted when he continued to walked up to the back of the house without making any moves toward her hiding place. She hadn't been spotted. Her relief, however, was short lived because was making a beeline for the door to the cellar. He pulled a flashlight from his cargo pants, and then disappeared into the same hole where Mr. Giles had gone. She was hopeful that her beloved feline companion would somehow manage to escape undetected. Her nerves were on edge as Susan held her breath, waiting for Mr. Giles to return. One anxious moment followed another until she felt like she had to do something. Just when she was about to throw caution to the wind and venture in after the mystery man, she heard the reassuring purr of a cat right behind her. Mr. Giles! She swiveled immediately, picked up the cat, and turned to make a break for the street. Immediately, the cat turned to glare at her, his intense eyes bored into hers. Jingles hissed his disapproval then instantaneously reached his claws out to attack.

"Ahh!" Susan yelped aloud amidst blocking her face with her hand. Despite her efforts, Jingles made contact, breaking the flesh on her hand with his sharp claws. She considered dropping him to the ground, but if that weren't enough to make his ire subside then she would be surrendering the only advantage she held in this battle. Formulating a plan to extricate herself from the combative feline while defending herself simultaneously was proving to be a losing combination. She considered a counter attack, but rapidly dismissed the idea. Even though she felt like she was in imminent danger, she still did not have the heart to cause any serious injury to a cat. Besides, she was prowling around in his territory; he had every right to attack her. Jingles obviously felt the same way, because his hairs stood on end as he hissed and swung at her menacingly. This time he caught her shirt between his claws, ripping the soft cotton to ribbons. Jingles clung to her shirt with his fore legs and swung wildly toward her mid-section with his hind legs. With much effort she managed to move him away from her body and fling him toward the backyard. After she let him go, he let out a loud kitty scream as he sailed away, his arms continuing to flail at her.

Susan thought it was impossible that this encounter had failed to attract anyone's attention. She expected Rosa or the mysterious stranger to appear at any moment to investigate the commotion. She attempted to flee the scene before she was discovered. Jingles, on the other hand, was not ready to discontinue his assault. He had efficiently covered the distance between them and was shredding the left leg of her jeans. , Happily the jeans were doing a remarkable job of providing protection for her flesh, preventing the angry cat from drawing blood for several seconds. Though Susan believed she could make it to her bicycle with him on her leg, she made repeated attempts to shake him loose. And the street looked further away with each stride.

Suddenly, the pressure on her leg had subsided and Jingles fell silent. Susan turned around to try to locate her assailant, when she spotted a most welcome sight. Mr. Giles! He had locked eyes with Jingles, diverting his attention. Susan backed away cautiously as Mr. Giles began playing with something she couldn't make out, but it was distracting the other cat. Susan followed her cue and took off for her bicycle, she had sprinted halfway across the yard when she heard a voice. It was a human voice. The shock of it almost stopped her heart.

"Well, what do we have here?" a male voice bellowed. Heavy footsteps were rapidly approaching.

Was this the way it would all end?

CHAPTER 10

Susan swiveled around to find herself looking directly into the eyes of Frank Matthews. "What are you doing here?" he demanded irritably.

"I have a perfectly good explanation for why Mr. Giles and I are here," she began speaking slowly while she thought of the best to back up the statement she was making.

"I'm not interested in your version of events, because I already know why you're here. You"—he pointed at her as if she were the evil he was here to fight against—"are interfering with our investigation. Our official police investigation. I should arrest you for obstructing justice."

Susan was indignant. "Me? Obstructing justice? That is the exact opposite of what I am doing. Do you realize that Mr. Giles and I have found almost every clue that you had on this case? We even found out where your mystery suspect is located right now."

"Really?" Frank's voice dripped with sarcasm. "Where?"

Susan led him to the underground lair of the man she suspected was David Marrin.

Frank went directly into cop mode. "Find Kip," he mouthed to her, waving her away with his hands. Stealthily, he approached the moss-covered wooden door, and then disappeared underground. Susan was just about to turn the corner to the front of the house, when she heard yelling from below. So she ran the rest of the way until the front door was in view. Kip was searching the living room with the door wide open. Screaming for Kip did not appear to be the best option, though, even if she could see him right through the screen door.

Susan flung open the screen door. "Detective Fletcher!" she called then scurried toward Kip to whisper into his ear. "Detective Matthews is in the back, he asked me to get you. He went down into a wooden door. I heard an argument."

"Stay here," he said to Susan. "I'm arresting anyone who moves," he stated meaningfully toward Rosa. Then he handcuffed her right hand to the railing of the banister for good measure.

After Kip left, the women eyed each other warily. Susan prayed Rosa did not try to escape. She did not want to get into her second fight of the night. Her body still ached from the first one.

Rosa spoke first, "I guess I don't have to ask why you're here," she stated bemusedly. "Looks like Jingles took a few chunks out of you." Rosa laughed a humorless laugh. "I warned you that he was territorial. Looks like you found out the hard way."

Ultimately Susan wanted to keep Rosa calm until Frank or Kip returned. She contemplated her options. Was it best to keep her talking? Or remain silent so as not to provoke her? Finally, she decided to respond with something non-confrontational.

"Yeah, you have yourself a good guard cat there," her tone was conciliatory. Maybe it would be enough to diffuse the tension in the room.

"I'm thinking of coming over there and finishing the job that jingles started. I have been daydreaming about tearing you to shreds." Rosa moved closer to her.

"You can't do that. You're handcuffed."

"About that." Rosa smirked. "This banister is old. We busted it up pretty good when we were kids. My dad stopped getting it repaired. Half of the rails on here are super-glue and sawdust." To prove her statement, she gave the rail a few firm yanks and it fell harmlessly onto the floor.

"You don't want to try anything." Susan did her best to sound convincing. "The cops will be back here any minute now." Susan added that last part mainly to reassure herself.

"Do you really think they'll get here in time to save you?" Rosa snapped back menacingly.

Susan was wondering the same thing. Her original plan, to keep Rosa calm, was clearly not going to work. Rosa was already agitated, so it was time to switch gears. If there was anything she remembered from grade school about bullies, it was that they fed on fear. Since that was the case, there was nothing to be gained by backing down.

"Are you planning to talk me to death or did you have something else in mind?" Soon she would know whether or not Rosa was making empty threats. "Either way you are not leaving this room."

Rosa made a move toward her, but Susan was quicker than she anticipated. A quick pivot to the left caused Rosa's fist to narrowly miss Susan's nose. Susan managed to grab a nearby vase in time to make contact with the side of Rosa's neck. Rosa was shaken by the blow, she stumbled back, momentarily dazed. Susan quickly took another swing trying her best to deliver a head shot. Unfortunately, Rosa was ready for it. She blocked Susan's arm, grabbed it, and then twisted Susan into a pretzel in front of her. Rosa, who was much stronger than she looked, soon had her opponent in a headlock. Susan attempted to pull her toward the exit and make an escape, but all her efforts were to no avail.

Susan writhed in pain. The pressure on her vocal passages wouldn't allow her to utter the screams that might signal her distress to someone who could help. All she could manage were gasps for air. As the seconds ticked by, she began to feel dizzy. Then Susan realized that by continuing to struggle she may have inadvertently been helping Rosa to support her weight.

Susan decided to let her body go limp, making Rosa support her full weight alone. Rosa fell back against the wall for support, "Had enough, have you?"

No response.

"Good." After Rosa loosened her grip around Susan's neck, Susan crumpled to the floor. Rosa immediately started for the exit. Susan was still dazed, but she knew now was the time to act. Susan willed herself to a standing position grabbed a coffee table and swung with everything she had. The coffee table hit Rosa on the shoulder and neck, knocking her sideways to the floor. Rosa lay motionless on the floor moaning, but she was mumbling and cursing by the time that Kip had returned.

Kip sized up the situation in the living room very quickly. His anger was thinly veiled. Rosa was now going to experience the joys of police custody. Kip handcuffed her wrists together, and then led her to the most uncomfortable looking chair he could find. A stiff wooden armchair that sat near the staircase was the one he selected. Kip pulled up a piece of the wicker sectional couch, and then slammed it on the floor directly in front of Rosa. He settled into his seat, glaring at his suspect the whole time. Susan sat as far away from the two of them as the room would allow. Mr. Giles picked that moment to enter the room and leapt into her arms. Susan softly stroked his fur, feeling at ease for the first time that night. Rosa's situation, however, had taken a turn in a different direction.

"Maybe I didn't make myself clear the last time I gave you a direct order," Kip hissed the words through clenched teeth. "I will try to be crystal clear this time. Now is the time for you to tell me the truth," he stated to Rosa, emphasizing each word. "Because after I take you downtown and lock you up, I'm going to lose interest in hearing your side of the story."

Rosa's defiance was fading fast. "I have the right to remain silent," she managed in a voice barely above a whisper.

"That is true. But your accomplice is outside with my partner right now and I'm willing to bet that he is singing like a canary. And do you know why? Reason number one is that Detective Matthews is very persuasive. He is especially convincing when he is angry. And right now, he is livid. Reason number two is that we have a preponderance of evidence that points directly at you stealing that tiger. And as soon as we get the fingerprints off of your little friend outside, we're going to nail him too. Reason number three, and my personal favorite, is that if I should have any trouble making my case, I have brand new charges to file against you. Because I have personally witnessed both of you committing felonies tonight. So the two of you can rot in jail while I put the pieces of my original case together."

"I don't know everything," Rosa insisted.

"My patience is wearing thin, Rosa. I've got both of you on resisting arrest and assault. I've got your buddy on assaulting a police officer. "Rosa's eyes grew wider with each new charge, "We've got obstructing justice, aiding and abetting—"

"Ok," she interrupted. "No new charges and I'll tell you what you want to know."

"No deal. My partner is pissed off. He really got worked over tonight, his jaw might be broken. And don't get me started on that cat of yours." He directed his finger and his glance toward Susan. "Ms. Becker and I will probably need tetanus shots." Eyes back on Rosa. "Honestly we could be talking about some civil charges here, too."

Rosa looked defeated. "Fine. I'll tell you what I know. It started when David faked his death, I was going to be his beneficiary, and we were going to split the money. It was supposed to be a piece of cake, but he had some opportunistic family members that came out of the woodwork to contest the will."

Rosa's voice conveyed naked contempt for these vultures who would dare to hijack their insurance scam. Kip nodded as if what she was saying made perfect sense.

"So David came up with a new plan." Rosa continued. "This was supposed to hold us until the insurance money was released from probate. He wanted to use his expertise to steal a rare animal; he said interested buyers had approached him on more than one occasion. He had kept contact information, just in case. David was setting everything up with the buyer. My job was to arrange a place to hold the animal after he was snatched. He and a guy named, Kyle Brenner, were supposed to be taking the tiger. Kyle was our inside man, he was integral to the plan. Everything was going according to plan, when Kyle got cold feet and wanted out. David went to talk to him, but it was clear that Kyle was not going to come around. So we needed a new plan for taking the animal off of the premises and transporting him to the holding area. David stole some of Kyle's stuff while he was there, so that we could move the tiger out of there without Kyle. He stole the meds to sedate the tiger, and then he drugged the security guards. That last guard came out of nowhere. I really don't know what happened to him---"

"You don't know what happened to him?!" Kip barked angrily. "What happened to him is that he had a heart condition and you shot him full of tranquilizers!" Kip's eyes locked onto Rosa's, "You killed him. That's what happened."

Rosa shook her head. "No, not me. That was David. He also sedated Kyle, so he wouldn't have an alibi during the heist. David thought we might need him later to take the fall if things started to go sour. It's really his fault. When he backed out of the heist at the last minute, that's when everything went haywire."

Kip veiled his exasperation, "How exactly did you get the tiger out of there?"

"Like I said we planned the whole thing with an insider. Kyle told us everything we needed to know about how to get this tiger, including which vehicle they use to transport her. It's a truck with lifts that places the cage right inside. We didn't want to scare her and risk attracting attention. We gave her the sedative right after we got her in the truck. It took awhile to work, but by the time we arrived at the fairgrounds, she was asleep. So we knew she wouldn't make a scene. We unloaded her, then we returned the truck right back to the spot where we found it."

"Well, that answers some of my questions. Where is Zena now?"

"I don't know. David never told me. He said he was protecting me."

"Well, I'm sure it was wise to listen to him. He sounds like a very trustworthy guy," Kip responded drily. He stood up. "Get up." He commanded Rosa, guided her to her feet, then led her out of the door. Soon Susan was alone in the room.

Secretly, Susan was enjoying the spectacle of watching Kip question a suspect. She thought there was something particularly attractive about this authoritative side of him. A man who knew how to take control was sexy, as long as he wasn't trying to take control of her.

As Susan rose to her feet, Mr. Giles jumped down onto the floor to lead the way to the exit. He must have read her mind. He disappeared out the front door. She found Mr. Giles on the side of the house near to the spot where he had been playing with Jingles. In his paws, she saw that he recovered his precious trinket from behind the bushes alongside the house. Then he followed her to her bike and settled into the basket. Mr. Giles began busying himself with his shiny trinket while Susan paid more attention to pedaling her aching body home.

When she arrived at her apartment, she dragged her weary body up the wooden steps. The creaking stairs sounded the way that her body felt—worn, weary and tired. The ride across town had not helped matters any.

Mr. Giles went off to carry his new shiny treasure to put in his treasure jar. Susan carried her aching body into the house and made a beeline for her own treasures, her shower and her bed. Susan allowed the shower to massage her aching body for at least half an hour, then dragged herself out and discarded her torn clothes into a heap on the floor. Her 4-poster bed beckoned. She couldn't wait to get in it, not even to observe her nightly ritual of combing her hair a hundred times as her grandmother had trained her to do. "Sorry, granny," she mumbled and then drifted off to sleep.

CHAPTER 11

Susan was eager to read the newspaper the following day. She just knew that in a small town like Lakeside the story of this case would be front page news. And she was right. She hoped her name wouldn't be mentioned. Investigating is a lot easier to do when people don't know you're doing it.

THE CASE OF THE MISSING BENGAL TIGER

On Thursday, August 3rd, in the middle of the night, a white Bengal tiger named Zena was abducted. A B & B employee named James Dennison was killed during the theft. The next morning, the B & B staff found Mr. Dennison's body and saw that their prize animal had vanished. Lakeside's finest believe that it must have been an inside job. Much of the early attention was given to Kyle Brenner, Zena's trainer, as a possible suspect. However, the plot that would soon unravel turned out to be far more complicated than that.

Unfortunately for Brenner, he had no alibi for the time in question. Subsequently, the evidence in the case continued to mount against him. All he had was a very odd story about a zoologist who he believed may be involved in the tiger's disappearance. His story would grow increasingly improbable with each new piece of evidence that surfaced against him. Brenner claimed to have received a ransom note to pay for

Zena's safe return. Later the police recovered a mountain of evidence in his own trailer, including the magazines that had been used to compile the ransom note.

The police would soon be shocked to learn that Kyle Brenner had been telling the truth all along. He had indeed been drugged so that he wouldn't have an alibi, while the two perpetrators had been busy abducting the tiger. The ransom note had been sent to him to cause him to leave his trailer so that the real criminals could plant evidence at his place. And probably the strangest part of all, the whole scheme had been dreamed up by a dead man.

David Marrin, a zoologist of Cincinnati, OH, has been presumed dead for several weeks. Lakeside police, however, have found him to be very much alive and living with his cousin, Lakeside resident, Rosa Dinkins. Allegedly, the two have been working together to abduct Zena and frame Kyle Brenner for the crime. Their motive was the money they could make selling a white Bengal tiger on the black market. As it turns out the price for such an animal is attractive indeed. One unverified account stated that Zena was to be sold for upwards of 1 million dollars to a private owner offshore.

Ms. Dinkins has confessed to the police about her participation in this crime. She has negotiated a reduced sentence with the district attorney and is currently out on bail. Details of the sentencing for Ms. Dinkins have not been made public as of this date. According to the district attorney, Ms. Dinkins' deal will remain sealed and off the record pending her testimony in Mr. Marrin's trial. Ms. Dinkins claims to have no knowledge about the whereabouts of the tiger.

Mr. Marrin has not admitted any culpability in the heist. He maintains his innocence and plans to stand trial. In addition to the charge of felony murder, Marrin faces a variety of charges, including armed robbery and aggravated assault. Bail for this defendant was strenuously opposed by the district attorney. In Mr. Marrin's arraignment, the judge agreed with the D.A. that Marrin is a flight risk. He has been remanded to custody in Miller County Jail pending trial. A trial date had not been set for his case at the time of this printing.

Zena, the tiger, has still not been recovered. B & B circus is offering a cash reward of $25,000 to the person or persons responsible for information leading to her safe return.

Susan noticed some inconsistencies between her personal knowledge of events and the summary available in the newspaper. For instance, apparently the reporter was unaware that Kyle was originally involved in the scheme to abduct Zena. To Susan's way of thinking it was better that this fact was not being made known; Kyle had done the right thing in the end. The poor guy was probably racked with guilt over the death of James Dennison. Something else she found of particular interest about this account was not only what was missing from it, but what had been added to it. There was a cash reward.

CHAPTER 12

Obviously, she had been wondering where Zena was since this whole thing began. As soon as she had finished reading the newspaper, she again pondered the possibilities of where Zena might be. Mr. Giles interrupted her thoughts by climbing out through the window. She often wondered why she had bothered with the pet door for him, when he continued to use the window. She thought absentmindedly on this as she heard the crack of her back staircase followed by a knock at the door. She peeped through the peephole to find Kip on the landing.

"Good morning, Kip! This is a surprise."

"Have you seen this?" he asked with the newspaper in his hand.

"Of course, you know I like to read the paper first thing after we close a case."

"We've got to go find Zena before anyone else does," he insisted.

"Haven't you already been looking for her?"

"Of course, we have and we were going to find her. These reporters are a menace to society. A cash reward?! It's a public safety hazard having civilians tracking a wild animal and who knows what kind of thug will be there with the tiger if someone does find him."

"That's true. If you did find her would you be eligible for that reward money?

"No, I can't receive a reward for doing my job. I don't think you understand what a nightmare this will be. Like I don't have enough problems trying to keep the peace in this town without a bunch of tiger hunting yahoos filling the streets!

"Well, I'm game. Where do you think we should start?"

"Go through everything that you have. Comb over it. If you think of anything that might tell us where this tiger might be, call me. If you or that cat of yours has any tricks up your sleeve, now's the time to pull them out."

Mr. Giles picked that moment to jump in through the window. It was as though he knew what was being discussed and did not want to be left out. She talked to him about places that a tiger could be kept. As a hobbyist spelunker, she considered a cave. Then she discounted that theory. How would the person get there with a truck? Each idea that popped into her mind was just as quickly discounted for some equally practical reason. Certainly, David had the good sense to get Zena out of Lakeside by now. While Susan pondered these possibilities, Mr. Giles pawed at his treasure jar, until he had captured Susan's attention.

"What's going on, Mr. Giles?" Seemingly agitated, he continued to paw at the jar. Susan pulled the items out and laid them on her bench seat for Mr. Giles to see "What are you looking for, boy?"

Now she had laid out all the shiny trinkets that had recently drawn the attention of Mr. Giles. All she saw were a number of odds and ends. Was there something here that had something to do with Zena's disappearance? Mr. Giles obviously felt that his job was done, because he was licking the back of his front paws and offering her no assistance whatever. She remembered that he had carried something back from Rosa's house last night. What was it?

She studied each item that lay before her. There was a button, which she recognized as being from her winter coat. There was an earring. She had been looking for that! Then she saw a gold plated key chain. Well, here was something that did not look familiar to her at all. She picked it up and read the name "North American Savings and Trust" emblazoned on the front. Now this was interesting. Susan vaguely remembered from a radio story she'd heard awhile back that a lot of criminals don't use offshore accounts like you see in the movies. The story said that there were plenty of banks with very attractive terms and banking policies right here in the U.S.A. Maybe this was one of those banks. This keychain was certainly not from a bank that she had visited. So if this were what Mr. Giles had brought back from Rosa's house, this could be a lead as to where David Marrin was keeping his ill-gotten gains.

Susan picked up her cell phone to call Kip back. Kip sounded cautiously optimistic about the value of this clue. He was mainly concerned that she wasn't 100% sure where the keychain. But he thanked her for her call and promised to let her know if anything came of it. Susan kept her expectations low when he mentioned something about a wild goose chase.

For the next several days everything went along as normal. Each time she saw Kip he had nothing new to report. Then on a Wednesday morning, Kip walked into her bakery with a huge smile on his face.

"It wasn't easy, but we found Marrin's account and tracked the payments. We contacted a middleman who gave up the location where Zena was being held. Zena was recovered from the docks in Miami. She is going back to B & B today. "

"What happened to the buyer?"

"Nothing. He never showed up. He must have been tipped off by somebody in advance."

"Tough break."

Kip shrugged. "You win some, and you lose some. I'm happy getting the crooks who nabbed the tiger and returning Zena back to her home. But I've got some good news for you."

"Do tell."

"You remember the reward money put up by B & B? Well, I told them that your tip broke the case for us so that we could recover the tiger. They want to cut you a check."

"Wow! Really?"

Kip was still talking, but Susan's mind had already drifted off on the vacation of a lifetime. She'd been daydreaming about it long enough. Mentally she began to weigh the pros and cons of the all the far flung travel destinations that occupied a place on her bucket list. Then she gave a conspiratorial look down at Mr. Giles who was standing guard by the door. She was about to come into a tidy sum of money, maybe the best way to resolve this inner conflict would be to visit them all.

Brand New Secret Wedding Planner Cozy Short Story Mystery Series by Janet Evans

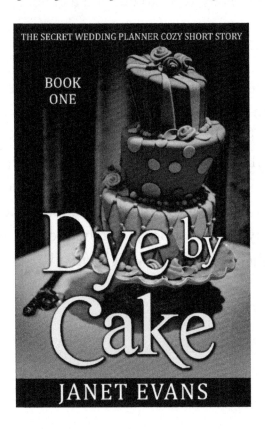

DYE BY CAKE – BOOK ONE

Groom Karl Stipple keels over moments after eating a slice of cake at his own wedding reception. Now the police have locked down the resort, and wedding planner Julia is under orders from her boss to solve the crime and clean up the mess in twenty-four hours-- or she's fired. It's a race against the clock as she finds herself entangled in a web of family mistrust, lingering old flames... and adult coloring books.

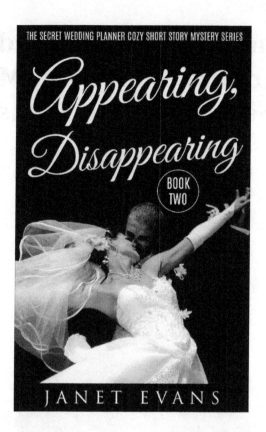

APPEARING, DISAPPEARING- BOOK TWO

For once, wedding planner Julia thinks a reception will go smoothly. Then the bride's heirloom diamond and gold engagement ring mysteriously vanishes. The police think they know who took it and have closed the investigation. It's up to Julia and her friends to save an innocent man from prison.

Brand New Secret Wedding Planner Cozy Short Story Mystery Series by Janet Evans

WEDDING SPLASH – BOOK THREE

It had been *exactly* 5 months, 4 days, and 16 weddings since the last mishap, and Julia was happy that finally, she got to plan a wedding where nothing terrible happened. This wedding is looking good. So far, no one tried to steal the bride's ring. No one tried to kill the groom.
She couldn't be more wrong. This one is the worst yet.